Tom Woof & Max The Owl

Jane Owen

D1198412

Once upon a time in the beautiful countryside, where there are rolling green hills, large leafy trees, and the bluest sky, was a farm with a thatched roof.

In one of the fields there was a huge beech tree that provided shade to the farm. It was also the home of the wisest of all the animals, Max The Owl, who watched over the farm from its top branches.

On the farm lived the most amazing animals, all different and special in their own way. Including 4 sheep, 6 pigs, 12 cows, 2 horses, 1 Owl (whom you have already met), and the newest addition to the farm, a little puppy called Woof, Thomas Woof.

Even though all the animals lived together, they didn't get along and fought with each other all the time.

The cows grumbled "Mooooo" at the sheep. The sheep bleated complaining "Baaaas".

The pigs meanly "Oinked" at the chickens. The chickens were always cluck clucking "Cluck cluck" at the horses. And as for the horses, well they did not speak to anyone who wasn't a horse.

But even though they didn't get along with each other and were always fighting, they agreed on one thing... The new addition to the farm Thomas Woof, was a very naughty puppy! Tom Woof the puppy was a writer, he was always writing on everything, He wrote on the walls of the stables. He wrote on the fences in the fields. He wrote on the roof of the coop where the chickens slept at night.

He wrote anywhere where there was space to write! He even wrote on the sheep's wooly bellies and on the backs of the cows while they were sleeping. Tom Woof was a puppy who loved making up stories. Every day there were new ones popping into his head.

All the animals on the farm were angry with Tom for writing everywhere. They didn't realize that it was because Tom felt strongly that he had to write them down as soon as he thought of them, wherever he was, otherwise he would forget them. They thought he was just being naughty. Tom's stories were scrawled all over the farm, with words here and sentences there. The animals on the farm could not read his

stories properly because the sentences were not in the right order, and they were all in different places instead of in one.

All they saw was their walls covered in scribbles! They saw A BIG MESS! This made Tom Woof very unpopular. The animals didn't like him at all. They complained about him to the Farmer. They called him a "Vandal!" and a "Troublemaker!". "He must STOP!" They all cried.

Tom Woof was lonely. He'd hoped that he would have friends in his new home. He wished the other animals could understand the stories he was trying to tell them.

Tom Woof couldn't understand why he was in trouble all the time just for writing his stories. Until one day, Max The Owl found Tom sitting under the big beech tree looking very sad, and he decided to talk to him about it. "There there Tom Woof, you have a wonderful talent!" he said, patting Tom's back with his wing.

Max The Owl had flown all around the farm reading Tom's writing and had realized that when you read the words and sentences all together, they made a wonderful story.

"You are a very good writer", he said to Tom, "but you should try to organize your stories and write them down in a book so that the other animals can read and enjoy them instead of reading only bits of them here and there."

"I understood it was a story because I could fly and see EVERYTHING you wrote all together", said Max " The pigs, cows, sheep and horses cannot fly, young Thomas, so they can't understand. When you write them all together, they will become a great story everyone can enjoy" This made Tom Woof smile.

"But first, we need to clean up the mess you made," said Max.

Over some sunny days, and a few rainy ones too, Tom Woof started scrubbing the walls, fences and roofs, where he had been writing his stories in scribbled words all jumbled up before. The other animals watched him and were happy that he was cleaning the farm.

He even washed the tummies of the sheep and the backs of the cows!

After he finished cleaning, Max showed Tom how to write all his ideas down in one place, all together in a book. He explained that stories can have Heroes and Heroines and problems to solve.

Max taught Tom how to decide what part of the story should go at the start, in the middle and at the end. He showed him how to write

a story down from start to finish, so that he could read them to the other animals, and to the Farmer and his family. When Tom had written his whole story down, all that was left was the title.

He called it "My New Home" and it was to be the first story in the Big Book of Stories by Tom Woof.

Max gathered all the animals together to listen to Tom Woof reading his first story. The animals were curious, "What did Tom Woof really have to say with all his writing here and there?" they asked each other. The sheep came, the cows came, the pigs, chickens and even the horses showed up to hear the story.

When they were all together, Tom stood in front of them and started to read his story out loud. It was wonderful, the animals laughed at the funny parts, gasped at the exciting parts, and hugged each other during the one scary part. When Tom finished reading his story, all the animals began applauding very loudly and congratulated him on writing such a good story!

Then they realized that this was the first time they had all been together without fighting! The pigs were not meanly oinking at the chickens, and the horses were finally talking to the other animals. Every evening from then on, Tom would read a new story to the animals, who were now his friends. They all enjoyed his stories so much that they would gather together the next day to talk about them. Sometimes they would discuss how the stories made them feel, and sometimes they would just talk about how excited they were to hear the next one. Some of them even started writing down their own stories.

Max and Tom wrote lots of stories together in the big book of stories and were best friends forever, on what was now a very happy and peaceful farm. After a while, the farm was renamed "Storybook Farm" and animals from all around came to visit, and to hear the stories Tom Woof would read to them.

To keep up with news about Tom Woof + Max The Owl
please visit www.tomwoof.com

Made in the USA
Middletown, DE
17 November 2020

24263054R00018